Peppa Pig™

Grampy Rabbit in Space

Peppa and her friends are at playgroup.
Today they have a special treat.
Grampy Rabbit is here to talk
about space rockets!

"Wocket!" snorts George. "Brrmm!"

"Hello, everybody!"
Grampy Rabbit shouts.
Grampy Rabbit
has a very
loud voice.

He holds up a
space rocket.
"It's a bit small!"
says Suzy Sheep.
"This is just a
model," explains
Grampy Rabbit.

"The rocket I went in was ginormous!"

Everyone gasps. Grampy Rabbit has flown to the moon in a space rocket!

Grampy Rabbit lifts the rocket into the air.
"When you go into space, you count backwards," he
says. "Five, four, three, two, one . . . BLAST OFF!"

Peppa and her friends all shout together.
"BLAST OFF!"

"There I was, flying through space," remembers Grampy Rabbit. "Ooh!" say the children.

VRROOOM!

"When I landed on the moon," says Grampy Rabbit, "it was so beautiful I was lost for words."
"That sounds nice," sighs Madame Gazelle.

Grampy Rabbit goes on. "Did you know that when you're on the moon you can jump as high as a house?"

Suddenly something strange happens.
Grampy Rabbit stops talking!

"Oh dear," says Madame Gazelle. "He has lost his voice."
Madame Gazelle asks Dr Brown Bear to come
and help Grampy Rabbit.

Dr Brown Bear looks into Grampy Rabbit's mouth. "I see," he says. "A very serious case of losing a voice."

The doctor pours some special
pink medicine on to his spoon.
"Open wide!" he says.

Grampy Rabbit swallows the medicine.

"Try saying 'ahh' now," says Dr Brown Bear.
The doctor listens carefully.

"AAAAHHHHHHH!" booms Grampy Rabbit.
The medicine has made his voice much better!

Grampy Rabbit gets back to his story.

"I wrote a song on the moon," he cries.
"Would you like to hear it?"
"No, thank you," say Madame Gazelle
and Dr Brown Bear.
"Yes, please!" say the children.

Twang!

"All together now . . ." sings Grampy Rabbit.

"I got up this morning,
I went to the moon,
And all I could see,
Was the moon and the stars!
The moon, the stars,
the moon, the stars,
the moon, the stars!"

Everybody loves
singing along with
Grampy Rabbit.